ANGEL CAT SUGAR

Star of the Ballet

By Ellie O'Ryan
Illustrated by Sachiho Hino

ANGEL CAT SUGAR
characters created by Yuko Shimizu

SCHOLASTIC INC.

New York Toronto London Auckland Sydney Mexico City New Delhi Hong Kong

ISBN 978-0-545-26635-2

12 11 10 9 8 7 6 5 4 3 2 1   11 12 13 14 15/0

Printed in the U.S.A. 40
First printing, January 2011

Angel Cat Sugar was getting ready.
Her dance school was having a ballet recital.
Everyone had a special job to do—especially Sugar.
She had the starring role!

Sugar had to practice her dance steps. She changed into her leotard and laced up her ballet slippers. "Now I just need my wand," she said.

Sugar twirled through the room, waving her wand as she danced. "I feel like a real ballerina!" she said.

When Sugar finished practicing, she visited Basil in the costume room.
"Hi, Basil," Sugar said. "How are the costumes coming along?"
"Okay, I guess," Basil replied. "Sewing takes a long time."

"Let me help," Sugar offered. Together she and Basil pointed their wands. *Whoosh!* Sparkling stars filled the air as Basil's sewing supplies turned into a beautiful tutu!

Next Sugar and Basil looked for Parsley. He was working on the set in the auditorium.

Parsley looked a little worried. "I hope I have time to finish painting the castle."

"We can help," Sugar suggested. The three friends waved their wands over the castle. *Whoosh!* The sparkles filled the set with beautiful colors!

"Now let's find Thyme," Sugar said.

Thyme was in the art room. He had made flyers to tell everyone about the ballet. "Now I have to hand them out all over town," he said.

"That sounds like a big job—but using our wands will make it easier," Sugar said. Together the friends waved their wands. *Whoosh!* The flyers fluttered out the window and landed in every mailbox on Misty Mountain.

The next night, it was time for the ballet! Sugar put on her tutu and ballet slippers. From backstage, she could hear the audience talking and laughing. Sugar started to feel a little nervous. *I hope I don't forget my dance steps,* she worried.

When the curtain opened, music started to play. Sugar held her wand tightly as she danced, and she didn't forget a single step!

At intermission, Sugar slipped backstage to see her friends.
"Great job, Sugar!" Basil squealed as she gave Sugar a big hug.
Parsley and Thyme crowded in to hug Sugar, too.

As Sugar hugged her friends, she accidentally dropped her wand. *Crack!* Her wand was broken!

"Oh, no!" Sugar cried. "I can't dance without my wand!"

"But you *have* to," Parsley replied. "Everybody's waiting for the rest of the ballet!"

"I'll fix it as quickly as I can," Basil promised. "Then you can dance over to get it for the rest of the show."

Sugar slowly walked toward center stage and waited for the curtain to open. She took one last peek at her friends. Thyme whispered, "You can do it, Sugar!"

But Sugar wasn't so sure. *How will I dance without my wand?* he wondered.

Then the curtain opened. As Sugar started to dance, something amazing happened. She leaped and twirled better than ever before! Sugar realized that her wand didn't make her a better dancer—all the time she spent practicing did!

"I fixed your wand!" Basil whispered. "But you don't need it. Your dancing is wonderful!"

"I don't need my wand to dance," Sugar whispered back. "But I do need it for something!"

Sugar twirled into the center of the stage holding her wand high. Rainbow stars scattered over the audience, making the whole room sparkle! Everyone cheered for the star of the ballet—Angel Cat Sugar!